## and the
# THREE
# ANGRY
# BEARS

For Morgan
R.I.


For Finley and Fred
K.M.

ORCHARD BOOKS

First published in Great Britain in 2016 by The Watts Publishing Group

1 3 5 7 9 10 8 6 4 2

Text © Rose Impey 2016

Illustrations © Katharine McEwen 2016

A CIP catalogue record for this book is available from the British Library.

ISBN 978 1 40832 521 6 (HB)
ISBN 978 1 40832 527 8 (PB)


Printed in China

MIX
Paper from
responsible sources
FSC® C104740
www.fsc.org

The paper and board used in this book are made from wood from responsible sources


Orchard Books
An imprint of Hachette Children's Group
Part of The Watts Publishing Group Limited
Carmelite House, 50 Victoria Embankment, London EC4Y 0DZ

An Hachette UK Company
www.hachette.co.uk
www.hachettechildrens.co.uk

# SIR LANCE-A-LITTLE

## and the

# THREE ANGRY BEARS

## Rose Impey · Katharine McEwen

ORCHARD

# Cast of Characters

Sir Lance-a-Little

Harold the Horse

Princess Plum

Huffalot the Dragon

Big Bear

Middle-sized Bear

Little Bear

The sun was shining. The birds were singing. Sir Lance-a-Little was thinking, *This is the perfect day to fight a dragon.*

He rode off on his trusty horse,
Harold, carrying his sharpest
sword, and his shiniest shield, and
his pointiest lance.

"Wait for me!" a voice called.
But Sir Lance-a-Little had no time
for his troublesome little cousin.
That low-down dragon, Huffalot,
would be waiting for him.

"Oh, bother, bother," grumbled Princess Plum. Determined not to be left behind, she set off running through the woods.

She didn't give a thought for anyone she might meet on the way.

That very morning, the dragon had received Sir Lance-a-Little's latest challenge.

HUFFALOT!
EXPECT ME EARLY!
YOU HAVE
BREATHED YOUR
LAST!

SIGNED:
YOUR NO1 ENEMY,
SIR LANCE-A-LITTLE

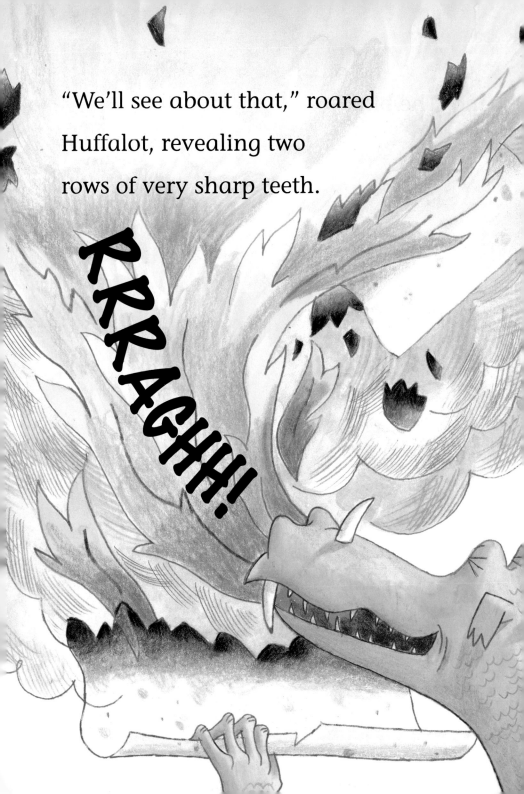

"We'll see about that," roared
Huffalot, revealing two
rows of very sharp teeth.

RRAGHH!

Meanwhile, not looking where she was going, Princess Plum ran smack bang into Three Angry Bears. "Someone's in a hurry," said the big bear.

"Looks like someone's up to no good," said the middle-sized bear. "Very red in the face," piped up the little bear.

Princess Plum had no idea what they were talking about.

Quite close by, Sir Lance-a-Little
was making very slow progress.
Harold was in one of his moods
and wouldn't be hurried.

Come on!

Suddenly, there was a kerfuffle
nearby. A familiar voice
was shouting, "But it wasn't me!"
Looking around, Sir Lance-a-Little
spotted his cousin
hiding up a tree.

Beneath the tree, the Three Angry Bears were waving their paws and growling.

"I didn't eat your porridge!" Princess Plum insisted.

16

"Well, someone did," said the big bear, "then ran away."

"You were running," said the middle-sized bear. "We saw you."

"I'm hungry," piped up the little bear. "Let's eat her instead!"

"Now, look here," Sir Lance-a-Little told the bears, bravely, "you can't eat her. She's my cousin."

But the bears didn't care whose
cousin she was. Still growling,
they surrounded Sir Lance-a-Little.
"Let's eat him up, too," the
little bear suggested.

Sir Lance-a-Little quickly climbed the tree to join his annoying cousin.

Oops!

"Now, what do we do?" she asked.

20

Sir Lance-a-Little looked down at the Three Angry Bears. They were clearly in no hurry.

"We can wait," said the big bear.

"All day if we have to," said the middle-sized bear.

"And all night," added the little bear.

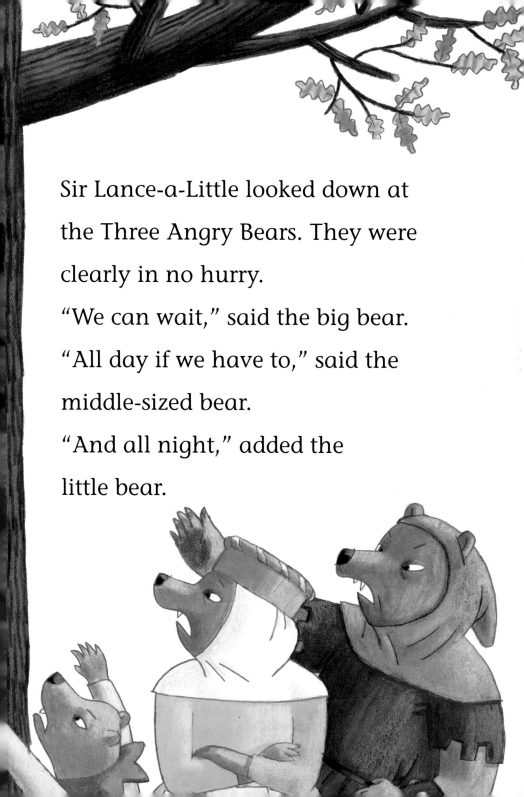

The dragon, on the other hand, had already given up waiting for Sir Lance-a-Little. He set off to find that unreliable knight and teach him a lesson.

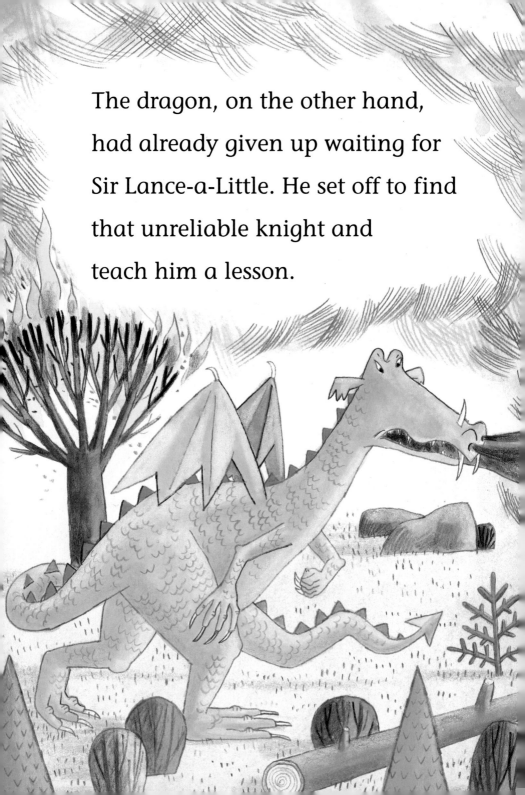

As Huffalot lumbered along,
he breathed out streams of fire,
setting light to trees as he went.

Sir Lance-a-Little and Princess Plum saw the flames and knew exactly who it was. But the bears didn't.

"Smells like burning," the little bear sniffed.

Burning!

"Maybe someone forgot to turn off the stove …" said Sir Lance-a-Little. "After they made the porridge," added Princess Plum.

The Three Angry Bears set off

home at a run.

"That was your job!" growled the

big bear.

"Why is it always my job?"

grumbled the middle-sized bear.

Sir Lance-a-Little quickly climbed down and looked for his sword. But, can you believe it, one of those rotten bears had run off with it.

*And* his pointy lance and his shiny shield had gone too! Even Harold, his not-so-trusty horse, had wandered off!

Sir Lance-a-Little felt rather nervous. Even the bravest knight in Notalot couldn't fight a dragon without a sword.

But, just then, the dragon
raced right past them,
chased by the Three
Angry Bears.
"I didn't set anyone's house
on fire!" he was
roaring.

Wait for me!

Sir Lance-a-Little turned for home.
"But what about the fight?" asked
Princess Plum.
"I think that can wait," he said
with a smile. "Huffalot seems to
be a bit busy right now."

THE
END

## Join the bravest knight in Notalot
## for all his adventures!

*Written by Rose Impey • Illustrated by Katharine McEwen*

❏ Sir Lance-a-Little and the
  Big Bad Wolf

978 1 40832 520 9 (HB)
978 1 40832 526 1 (PB)

❏ Sir Lance-a-Little and the
  Three Angry Bears

978 1 40832 521 6 (HB)
978 1 40832 527 8 (PB)

❏ Sir Lance-a-Little and the
  Most Annoying Fairy

978 1 40832 522 3 (HB)
978 1 40832 528 5 (PB)

❏ Sir Lance-a-Little and the
  Terribly Ugly Troll

978 1 40832 523 0 (HB)
978 1 40832 529 2 (PB)

❏ Sir Lance-a-Little and the
  Ginormous Giant

978 1 40832 524 7 (HB)
978 1 40832 530 8 (PB)

❏ Sir Lance-a-Little and the
  Very Wicked Witch

978 1 40832 525 4 (HB)
978 1 40832 531 5 (PB)

Orchard Books are available from all good bookshops, or can be ordered from our website:
www.orchardbooks.co.uk
or telephone 01235 400400, or fax 01235 400454.

Prices and availability are subject to change.